Jo's Storm

Caroline Pitcher
Illustrated by Jackie Morris

RED FOX

For Richard, Lauren and Max with love – CP
For Thomas Rainbow – JM

A Red Fox Book

Published by Random House Children's Books
20 Vauxhall Bridge Road, London SW1V 2SA
A division of The Random House Group Ltd
London Melbourne Sydney Auckland
Johannesburg and agencies throughout the world

1 3 5 7 9 10 8 6 4 2

First published in Great Britain by The Bodley Head Children's Books 1994

Red Fox edition 1999

Printed in Singapore

RANDOM HOUSE UK Limited Reg. No. 954009

ISBN 0 09 187306 1

When Jo cut paper snowflakes,

one fluttered up and whispered in his ear, 'Cut out my brothers, blinding white, and let them drift into the frozen night.'

Jo cut until his fingers numbed, and he stood
in a snowstorm of his own.

Snip Snap. Across the wastes he heard the slap-slap of bright
webbed feet, and through the storm there danced a penguin
party, whooping and sliding on the ice.

Jo cut them fish which leaped above the freezing sea. Snip Snap.
Up bobbed a sleek round head, a seal, who barked, 'Cut a
fish for me!'

Jo cut the fish and tossed it high to Seal who caught it and clapped flippers, 'Thank you, Jo.'

Snip Snap. In the corner of Jo's eye
loomed, ghost-like, a polar bear.
She dipped her great paw in the sea
as if she scooped out honey from a hive.
   'DIVE DIVE DIVE!' cried Jo, and Seal
was gone.

Polar Bear shook her head and growled, 'I'll breakfast on a penguin steak instead.'

So Jo Snip Snapped a ship to break the ice and send the penguins floating safely on a floe.

Bear grumbled, but from far away she heard her twin cubs cry, and lumbered off to comfort them from cold.

Up bobbed Seal and flopped across the snow, and Jo cut out a lemon-coloured sun so Seal could bask and he could doze.

Snip Snap. Penguins panicked and fell off their
floe as through the waves sliced Whale's dark hill.

And only Jo heard from the watery depths Whale's sad song, 'Save me from the whaling ship, the man with deadly harpoon gun. My calf is lost. My friends are gone.'

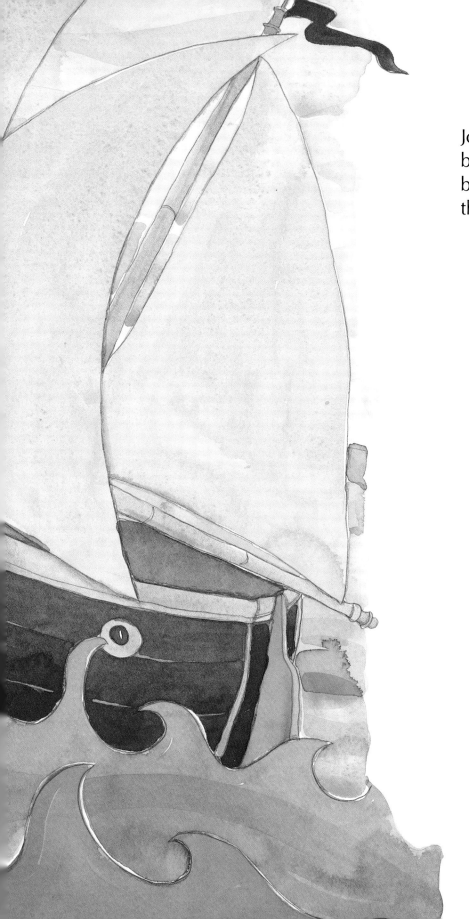

Jo sent his ship to smash the ice and block the whaler's way. He blew a blizzard of a million flakes to blind the hunter on the bridge,

then clambered up Whale's back to steer her out across the world,
and find her calf.

When they swam safely in their ocean home, Jo let his
snowstorm die away and, weary now, he curled up in
his chair and watched the snowflakes settle on the pane.